This Little Tiger book
belongs to:

_____

_____

_____

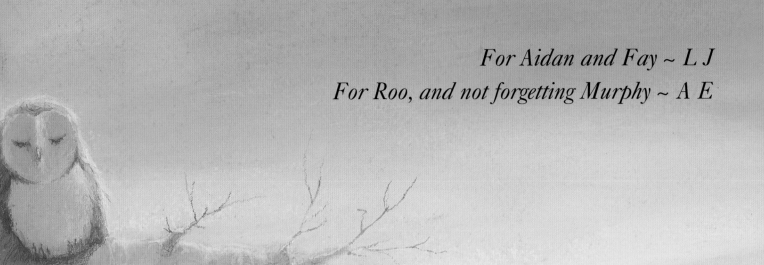

For Aidan and Fay ~ L J
For Roo, and not forgetting Murphy ~ A E

LITTLE TIGER PRESS
An imprint of Magi Publications
1 The Coda Centre, 189 Munster Road,
London SW6 6AW • www.littletigerpress.com

First published in Great Britain 2008
This edition published 2008

Text copyright © Linda Jennings 2008
Illustrations copyright © Alison Edgson 2008
Linda Jennings and Alison Edgson have asserted their rights
to be identified as the author and illustrator of this work under
the Copyright, Designs and Patents Act, 1988

A CIP catalogue record for this book is available from the British Library

Printed in China

3 4 5 6 7 8 9 10

Lost in the Snow

Linda Jennings

illustrated by Alison Edgson

LITTLE TIGER PRESS
London

Ollie peeped out of the barn door. Something cold and wet plopped on his nose. "What's all this white stuff, Mum?" he squeaked. "Can you eat it?"

"It's snow, Ollie," his mum laughed. "It falls like rain in winter. And no, you shouldn't eat it."

"Can we play in it, then?" he asked.

"Please, Mum," cried Sheba and Sam.

"Of course you can," said Mum, "but don't go too far."

Sam and Sheba skidded and slid
across the icy farmyard.
 "Wait for me!" yelped Ollie,
racing after them.

When the puppies reached
the field, they stopped and stared.
There was snow everywhere.
 "Let's play!" cried Ollie.

The puppies chased and dug
and rolled under the flying
snowflakes, until
suddenly . . .

. . . a strange face loomed up in front
of them – a face with a huge mouth,
huge eyes and HUGE teeth!

For a moment the puppies
froze with fear.
"RUN!" Sheba cried.

The puppies rushed off through the flurrying snowflakes. Ollie's paws scrabbled and skidded as he ran and ran, until at last the dog's barks faded and everything was quiet and still. But where were Sheba and Sam? Where were the farmyard and the barn?

"Oh no," whimpered Ollie.
"I'm lost!"

"Too whit, too whoo, who are you?"

hooted a voice high above him. Ollie looked up. Two big, round eyes stared down.

"I'm Ollie and I've lost my family and I don't know my way home," Ollie squeaked.

"Perhaps you should follow your footprints," suggested the owl. "They'll lead you home again – but hurry, or they'll be covered in snow."

"Thank you so much!" said Ollie. "I'll do that."

Tail wagging, he set off. But by the time he had reached the middle of the field, the footprints were disappearing under fresh snow. Soon Ollie couldn't see them at all.

He trudged on and on as the snow grew deeper. "I must keep going," he panted. "I *must* get back to my nice, warm basket and supper."

At last Ollie reached a large
wood. Was this the wood by
his farm? If it was, then he
was nearly home!

The snow had stopped, and evening
sunlight shone through the trees.
Crunch, crunch, Ollie crept
through the icy leaves. But then,
all at once . . .

Swoosh!

Ollie slipped down
an icy slope,

tumbling

over

and over . . .

THUMP!

From the shadow of the bushes
three fox cubs stared out at him.

"Look what the snow's blown in,"
said one.

"What a scruff!" said another.

"This is *our* home," said the third.
"Clear off!"

"But I don't know which way to go!"
cried Ollie. Sadly he walked away. He
would have to find his own way home.

Ollie reached the edge of the wood, but still he couldn't see the farm. He tried to cheer himself up. He'd have so much to tell Sam and Sheba when he reached home!

But the snow was falling once more, thicker and faster. As he struggled on, Ollie began to think he would never see his family again.

Cold, hungry, and very, very tired, Ollie
crawled under a bush.

A mouse scurried past his feet and
disappeared into a small hole. "I wish I
could find somewhere safe and warm to
sleep, too," Ollie sighed. But as he closed
his eyes, he heard something . . .

"Ollie! OLLIE! Where are you?"
Ollie peeped out from the bush –
it was Mum!

"Mum! Sam! Sheba! I'm over here!"
And across the frozen field Ollie
raced to meet them.

"We've been looking for you for hours,"
cried Mum. "Where have you been?"
"I've had an adventure," said Ollie.
"But I'm so glad it's over now."
"So am I," said Mum, gently licking
his freezing ears.

Home at last, Ollie curled up with his brother and sister in their cosy bed. The puppies wanted to know all about Ollie's Big Adventure.

"Tell us more about the owl!" cried Sheba.

"And the nasty fox cubs!" squeaked Sam.

But, warm and snug, his tummy full of dinner, Ollie had fallen fast asleep.

Snuggle up with these books
from Little Tiger Press

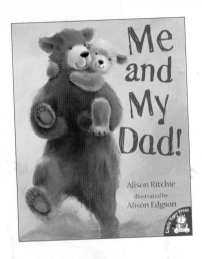

Me and My Dad!
Alison Ritchie
illustrated by Alison Edgson

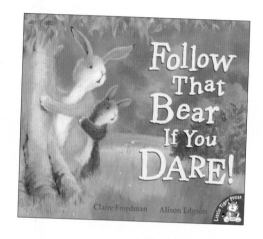

Follow That Bear If You DARE!
Claire Freedman Alison Edgson

Don't be Afraid, Little Ones
M Christina Butler Caroline Pedler

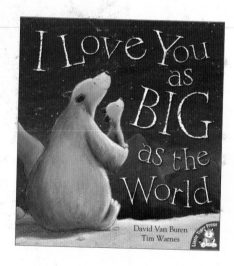

I Love You as BIG as the World
David Van Buren Tim Warnes

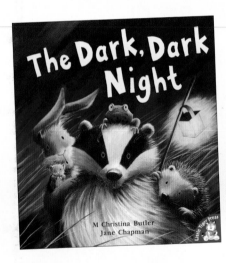

The Dark, Dark Night
M Christina Butler Jane Chapman

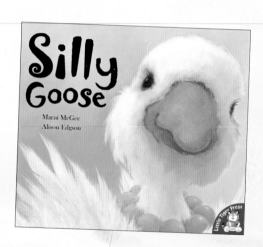

Silly Goose
Marni McGee Alison Edgson

For information regarding any of the above titles
or for our catalogue, please contact us:
Little Tiger Press, 1 The Coda Centre,
189 Munster Road, London SW6 6AW
Tel: 020 7385 6333 Fax: 020 7385 7333
E-mail: info@littletiger.co.uk www.littletigerpress.com